The Golden Goose King

A Tale Told by the Buddha

The Golden Goose King

A Tale Told by the Buddha

Retold and Illustrated by Judith Ernst

Foreword by Carl W. Ernst

Parvardigar Press

To Noor Inayat Khan for her love of
the Jatakas and her ultimate self-sacrifice;
to Carl, Tess, and Sophie for their endless love and support;
and especially to the memory of Mehera J. Irani for
her example of pure, selfless love.

The paintings in this book were done in Winsor & Newton Designers Gouache,
on 140 lb. Fabriano Artistico Cold Pressed 100% cotton mouldmade paper produced in Italy.
The book was printed in Singapore by Tien Wah Press on 115 gms Nymolla Matt Art Paper and
bound in Dynic Saifu. The book was designed and typeset by Kachergis Book Design of
Pittsboro, North Carolina on a Macintosh in Poetica Chancery II.

Copyright © 1995 by Parvardigar Press
Cataloging in Publication Data
Ernst, Judith.
The golden goose king : a tale told by the Buddha / retold
and illustrated by Judith Ernst.
p. cm.
Preassigned LCCN: 94-74107.
ISBN 0-9644362-0-5
1. Jataka stories, English. 2. Jataka stores. I. Title.
BQ1462.E5E 76 1995   294.3'823
QBI94-21242

Parvardigar Press, Post Office Box 4631, Chapel Hill, NC 27515

Foreword

"The Golden Goose King," a Buddhist Jataka Story

The religious movement initiated by Gotama the Buddha unleashed an unprecedented transformation across the face of Asia. In the following centuries, some of the most important cultural monuments of Asian civilization were inspired by Buddhism, and to this day it remains one of the major religions of the world, with hundreds of millions of adherents.

Among the literary and scriptural treasures of Buddhism, the Jataka texts hold a special place. The Jatakas consist of over five hundred stories about the previous incarnations of the Buddha in both human and animal form. The Jataka stories are told by the Buddha himself, and at the end of each story he identifies the role that he himself played, and sometimes the roles of others as well, particularly his disciples. The Jataka collections were transmitted orally for centuries, and when written down they took a form combined of verse, story, and moral commentary. The traditional belief is that they form part of the canon of Buddhist scriptures established in 483 B.C., at the council that his disciples held shortly after his death.

While the overall Buddhist flavor of the Jatakas is unmistakable, a number of these stories may previously have been part of non-Buddhist Indian narrative traditions. The question of the religious character of the Jatakas is complicated by the fact that quite a few of these stories have been exported through translation and detached altogether from the Buddhist context. Together with stories from another ancient Indian collection, the "Panchatantra," the Jatakas were translated through a bewildering series of languages—Persian, Arabic, Syriac, Georgian, Greek, Hebrew, French,

Spanish, and English. These versions were, however, transformed by their removal from the Buddhist canon; the frame story that located each tale in relation to the life of the Buddha, the underlying ideas of reincarnation and karma, and the identification of characters that ended each tale, were all cut away. What remained were entertaining and occasionally moralistic animal stories, but demythologized for a generic storytelling purpose. Only rarely did a religious aura remain, as in the unusual case of the story of Gotama's renunciation of the world, which in some versions portrayed him as a Christian saint. Still, it is remarkable that these "detached" Jataka stories have proven to be among the most widely popularized narratives in world literature.

In presenting this Jataka story as the first publication of Parvardigar Press, Judith Ernst reminds us of its placement as a sacred text, as part of the Buddhist canon. After the monumental translation from the Pali produced under the supervision of E. B. Cowell a century ago, almost every adaptation of the Jataka stories published in English has dropped the Buddhist frame stories. The result has been, like the medieval Near Eastern and European translations, a demythologized text, an animal fable, often written down to a juvenile level in accordance with modern marketing practice. While simplicity is doubtless part of the charm of the Jatakas, when viewed as narratives told by the Buddha they also contain an aura of transcendence, the "taste of the dharma." One of the achievements of this version of "The Golden Goose King" is to transport us not merely into the timeless world of the tale, where the dream of the queen of Benares leads to an encounter with the luminous and spiritual bird; this version also takes us to the second-order reflection on the tale, as the primordial anticipation in a previous life of the self-sacrificing love of Ananda for the Buddha.

"The Golden Goose King" is based on three similar and closely related stories taken from the Pali Jatakas (nos. 502, 533, and 534 in the Cowell version). All three have the same basic outline. The story begins with the Buddha's observation that his beloved disciple Ananda has on more than one occasion been ready to sacrifice his life for the Buddha. In the longest version, we hear how that day the Buddha's misguided opponent Devadatta had gotten a bull elephant drunk, intending that the beast should go on a rampage and kill the Buddha. Three times Ananda placed himself in front of the raging elephant to protect his master before the Buddha quietened it by revealing his cosmic status. He then related to his disciples the story of another lifetime, when he and Ananda were magnificent golden geese who were sought by the king and queen of Benares. An Indian audience would have recognized at once that the goose or "hamsa" was an ancient symbol for the soul liberated from the bonds of mortality.

In presenting this story in an illustrated form, Judith Ernst has invoked a rich ancient pictorial tradition. Before the advent of printing, illustrated books were the prerogative of connoisseurs and royal patrons. In Buddhist art, the Jatakas have been lavished with special attention over the centuries, often carved in stone in the great Buddhist monuments of India and Southeast Asia. In choosing a pictorial style for the Jatakas, one cannot ignore the paintings of the Ajanta caves in western India. These exquisite portraits convey all the elegance and calm appreciation of physical beauty that emerged from the courts of ancient India as depicted for a major Buddhist center fifteen hundred years ago. At Ajanta it is still possible to see a cave painting illustrating the very same story related in this book, though during a visit some years ago it was almost impossible to discern the figures due to deterioration. It is in the spirit of the art of Ajanta, with more than a nod to the physical textures and styles represented there and at other Buddhist monuments such as Sanchi, that Judith Ernst has undertaken the meticulous and lucid miniature paintings that accompany the text.

This book proposes to make available some of the richness of a narrative literature from one of the great religious and artistic traditions of Asia. It does so with sympathy and engagement, suggesting by demonstration the possibility of appreciating some of the inner depth of a culture that is not inherited. Today we have access in theory to all the great achievements of past cultures of every time and place, but too often our ability to take advantage of them is restricted by lack of information and opportunity. "The Golden Goose King" presents a story of love, beauty, and self-sacrifice, accessible to a modern audience but acknowledging the original cultural and religious context of the tale. It is hoped that readers of many different backgrounds and ages will find here a fragrance of the spirit that propelled Buddhist art and culture throughout the world.

Carl W. Ernst
Professor of Religious Studies
University of North Carolina at Chapel Hill

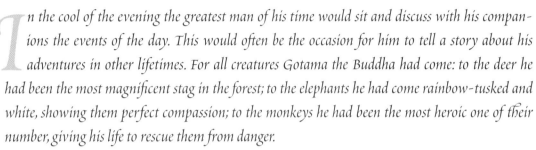

*I*n the cool of the evening the greatest man of his time would sit and discuss with his companions the events of the day. This would often be the occasion for him to tell a story about his adventures in other lifetimes. For all creatures Gotama the Buddha had come: to the deer he had been the most magnificent stag in the forest; to the elephants he had come rainbow-tusked and white, showing them perfect compassion; to the monkeys he had been the most heroic one of their number, giving his life to rescue them from danger.

One evening Gotama and his companions talked about an extraordinary event that had occurred that day. An enemy of Gotama had given liquor to a bull elephant and released the drunken and enraged animal into the Buddha's path. The disciple Ananda threw himself between the elephant and Gotama, only to be miraculously removed by the Buddha at the last moment. "You are a brute elephant, but I am the Buddha elephant!" declared Gotama to the maddened animal. Hearing this the elephant meekly bowed at the feet of the Buddha. After discussing these events with his companions, Gotama told this story of his life as a great golden goose.

Once upon a time when Samyama reigned in Benares with his Queen, Khema, the Buddha lived as the king of a flock of ninety thousand golden geese who dwelt on Mount Cittakuta. One morning just at daybreak, as the Queen lay in bed enjoying that state between sleeping and waking, she had a vision of two gold-colored geese. In her mind's eye she saw them perched on the royal throne, speaking sweetly to her. But soon she awoke, only to find that her vision had vanished. It had been just a dream. All that day she was troubled. The dream had seemed so real that she longed to hear once again the sweet voices of the geese, to feel their soft golden feathers beneath her fingers, and to feast her eyes on their great beauty. The more she dwelled on these thoughts, the more convinced the Queen became that these magnificent birds must indeed exist somewhere in the world. With this thought in mind, she went to her husband, the king, saying, "My Lord, I long to listen to the sweet speech of a golden goose, to feed it delicacies, present it with flowers, and pay homage to it. What can be done to fulfill my wish?"

The King, who loved his wife dearly and who would do anything to make her happy, consulted with his advisers and decided on a plan to capture a golden goose. A lake was built on the edge of the city to be a sanctuary for all birds. It was a lovely place, planted with five kinds of lotuses, and surrounded by various types of grains and fruits for the birds to feed upon. All sorts of birds flocked there, and the bees swarmed. People were not allowed to visit this paradise, for their presence would have frightened the birds. But one person was allowed to stay there: a skilled fowler, trained to know everything a human being could know about the habits of birds. It was he who was charged with the task of catching a golden goose.

After the lake had been established for some time, the different families of geese started to arrive. First came the grass geese, followed by the yellow geese. Then the yellow geese told the scarlet geese, and they told the white geese, who were followed by the paka geese. Now it so happened that the paka geese were related to the golden geese by marriage, and that is how the golden geese came to hear of the beautiful lake that was to become their feeding ground. One day Sumulkha, the captain of the Golden Goose King, who had been talking with some of the paka geese about this wondrous lake that had appeared near the city of Benares, went to the Goose King, saying, "Sire, we have heard of a new lake, so bountifully stocked that all of our geese can find more than enough to eat. I think we should fly there. What does My Lord say to my suggestion?"

Being an ancient and wise bird, the Goose King had experienced before the tricks of the human race, and he was understandably suspicious. "Why was there never before such a lake?" he asked. "This could be a trick. The lake might have been made just to capture us."

In spite of the king's reservations, he finally gave in to the wishes of his flock, who were all very excited about the prospect of visiting such a perfect place. So off flew the flock of ninety thousand geese to the lake, where they ate their fill, and then returned to Mount Cittakuta.

But while the geese had feasted at the lake the fowler had lain concealed in the bushes. As soon as the geese flew away, off he ran to report what he had seen to the King and Queen of Benares. They were greatly excited by the news, and the king said to the fowler, "The time has now come to capture one of these marvelous creatures. Remember! If you should catch a golden goose, great honor will come to you and your family!"

So the next day the fowler, expecting the geese to return, lay concealed in order to observe their movements. While huddled in the bushes unobserved, the fowler made a startling discovery. Most of the geese, wanting to eat the choicest morsels from the lake, moved quickly from place to place, afraid that they wouldn't get their share. But one of the geese, an especially large and beautiful one, stayed in one location and ate what was available there. Noticing this, the fowler thought, "This goose is not greedy. This is the one I must catch."

On the next day the fowler concealed himself close to the spot where the Goose King had alighted the previous day, and as anticipated, the bird came down in the same spot and continued eating where he had left off. Looking through a crack in his hiding place, the fowler for the first time got a close look at the great Goose King. To his amazement he saw a huge bird, as big as a wagon, gold-colored, with three red stripes encircling its neck. It had three red stripes running down its throat and along the middle of its belly, and three more red stripes running down and marking off its back. At this beautiful sight the fowler thought, "This bird shines like a lump of the purest gold bound by red silk thread. This must be their king, and this is the one I will capture."

For six days the geese fed in this manner, and for six days the fowler lay concealed, watching the Goose King as he ate, hoping to learn enough about his habits in order to anticipate the exact spot of his descent. On the seventh day the fowler made a snare of stout horse hair, and fixing it upon a stick, placed it where he now knew the Goose King would alight. As expected, the Goose King landed right where the snare was placed, thrusting his foot into the loop. It closed and held him fast!

At first the Goose King tried to break the band, but struggling caused the band to cut through the flesh of his leg. Thinking that it would not befit a king to have a maimed body, the goose ceased to struggle. The pain from the wound increased, but the king thought, "If I cry out now that I've been captured, my birds will all flee before they've finished eating, will be too weak to make the journey home, and will fall from the sky." So the king, suffering from the pain of his wound, pretended to be feeding until the entire flock had finished their meal. Only then did he shout the cry of capture. The geese all flew away in terror.

The sound of beating wings and terrified cries pierced the air. In the midst of this chaos the King's captain, Sumulkha, realized to his horror that his king was not with the rest of the flock. He raced back to the lake. There he found the beautiful goose caught in a snare, stained with blood and in great pain, lying on the muddy ground. Comforting the King, Sumulkha said, "Fear not, Sire! I will stay with you!" And as the two birds rested, calmly awaiting their fate, the fowler walked toward them, club in hand and his jaw set, planting his heel firmly in the mud as he reached his prey. But as he gazed at the two geese, it suddenly occurred to the fowler to wonder why the second goose, who was apparently free to go, had not fled.

Just at the moment when this thought came into the mind of the fowler, Sumulkha flew up to his lord's captor and, poised in the air, said in a sweet human voice, "Do not imagine, Friend, that an ordinary goose has been caught in your snare. You have captured the chief of ninety thousand geese. He is a king, ruling with virtue and wisdom. You must not take him. I too am gold-colored. If you desire his feathers, take mine; if you want to tame him, tame me instead; or if you wish to make money, make it by selling me. He is my king and I serve him. I cannot leave him to face an evil fate alone while I fly to safety."

Witnessing this extraordinary loyalty and devotion, the fowler was overcome and exclaimed, "What wise and holy creatures these are!" He dropped his club, and raising his joined hands to his forehead, stood joyously proclaiming the virtues of the two birds.

Tenderly approaching the wounded goose king, the fowler took him in his arms, laid him on some soft grass, and loosed the snare from his foot. Then feeling a great affection for the bird, the fowler carefully washed his wound. The power of the fowler's kindness and the greatness of the Goose King's character then caused the wound miraculously to heal, flesh uniting with flesh, skin with skin, and nerve with nerve. The great Goose King sat and rejoiced at his wounded foot once again made whole.

Sumulkha then asked the fowler why he had trapped the goose king in the snare. "I was employed by my lord Samyama, King of Benares," replied the fowler, and then he told them the whole story, from the time of the Queen's dream to the point seven days before when the King had ordered the fowler to catch one of the golden geese. Hearing this story gave Sumulkha an idea, and turning to the Goose King, he said in bird language, "Sire, this fowler has done us a great service. If he had not freed you he might have won great wealth. Let us go with him to see the King and Queen of Benares and thereby bring upon him great honor."

Turning to the fowler, in human speech he said, "Sir, we wish you to present us to your king, but do not take us as captives. Make a large cage shaded with white lotuses for my lord, the Goose King. For me, build a small cage covered with pink lotuses. Carry my king in front and me behind, somewhat lower. Take us quickly and introduce us to your lord."

So the fowler carried them in that manner through the streets of Benares, making his way toward the palace through crowds of people amazed at the sight of the two golden geese housed in lotus cages. At the palace door they were announced and then brought before the King of Benares, who upon seeing them exclaimed, "My heart's desire is fulfilled!"

The King ordered his courtiers to take the fowler and have his hair and beard trimmed, and have him bathed and dressed in the finest clothing. Afterward he was brought once again into the King's presence, and the King awarded him land, a chariot pulled by two of the finest thoroughbreds, a beautiful house, and much gold and silver, and bestowed upon him great honor. Abashed, the fowler sought to explain to the King what he had done. "Sire, this is no ordinary goose that I have brought to you. He is the king of ninety thousand geese and this other goose is his chief captain." Then the fowler told the King the whole story—how he had watched the geese feed for six days and noted the outstanding qualities of the Goose King; how he had then set a snare and caught the goose in the very place where he knew that he would alight and continue feeding; and how the goose captain had flown to his lord's side and had pleaded with the fowler for his king's life.

After hearing the fowler relate these wonders, the King offered to the Goose King a precious throne spread with costly Benares silk, and to Sumulkha he offered a golden chair covered with a tiger skin. Then he fed them both parched corn, honey, and molasses from golden vessels.

The King of Benares had been especially touched by Sumulkha's readiness to give up his own freedom for that of his master. So as the sun set, the lamps were lit, and Queen Khema entered, the King politely asked Sumulkha to speak to the assembly. To this request the goose captain replied, "I am a servant, my Lord. How could I speak, Sire, when to my left sits my king, wise and virtuous of character and beautiful to behold, while on my right sits the mighty King of Benares?"

On hearing this the King's heart was uplifted and he said to Sumulkha, "Sir, the fowler's praise of you was just. You are truly an example of loyalty and service to your lord. I must then turn my attention toward the source of your wisdom, toward your wise king and master." And turning toward the Golden Goose King, the King of Benares begged the bird to preach his wisdom to the gathering.

So the Golden Goose graciously entered into pleasant conversation with the Royal Couple, skillfully bringing into the talk the moral precepts that good kings and queens ought to rule by. The whole night the Golden Goose spent preaching the law, and when the sun was near to rising he asked permission of the King to leave with Sumulkha.

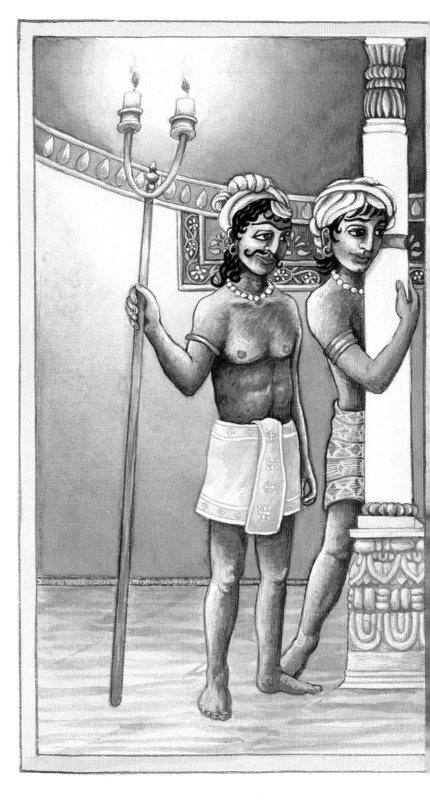

Once again the King served the birds in golden dishes, and then offering them scented wreaths, and paying great homage to them, the King himself lifted the Goose King and Queen Khema lifted Sumulkha. At the moment of sunrise they opened the window, and saying, "Sirs, away!" let them loose.

*A*s the Great Goose flew out of the window he stopped for a moment, poised in the air, and said to the King and Queen, "Good people, be not troubled by our leaving, but remember the moral laws that I have preached. Rule your kingdom righteously and win the hearts of your people." So saying, he flew away with Sumulkha and made straight for Mount Cittakuta where his flock of geese anxiously awaited his return.

After telling this story to his attentive audience, the Buddha explained that his chief companion, Ananda, had before been Sumulkha, the goose captain. Both as Sumulkha and as Ananda he had shown his loyalty and his willingness to sacrifice himself for the Buddha. Then the Buddha assigned the other parts of the story as follows: "At that time the fowler was my companion Channa; Queen Khema was the nun now also named Khema; the King of Benares was my companion Sariputta; and the Goose King was I myself." The Buddha concluded by saying,

"Thus all whose hearts are full of love succeed in
what they do,
Just as these geese back to their friends once more
in safety flew."